Abby

# Abby

By **Wolfram Hänel**

*Illustrated by* **Alan Marks**

*Translated by Rosemary Lanning*

**North-South Books**

*NEW YORK · LONDON*

First published in the United States, Great Britain, Canada,
Australia, and New Zealand in 1996 by North-South Books,
an imprint of Nord-Süd Verlag AG, Gossau Zürich, Switzerland.
Distributed in the United States by North-South Books Inc., New York.

Library of Congress Cataloging-in-Publication Data is available.
A CIP catalogue record for this book is available from The British Library.
ISBN 1-55858-648-2 (TRADE BINDING)
1 3 5 7 9 TB 10 8 6 4 2
ISBN 1-55858-649-0 (LIBRARY BINDING)
1 3 5 7 9 LB 10 8 6 4 2
Printed in Belgium

For more information about our books, and the authors and artists
who create them, visit our web site: http://www.northsouth.com

Far out at sea, off the Irish coast, lies an island. It is a very small island, with four fishing boats, and more sheep than people.

The people who live on the island don't have much time to sit and talk, except on Saturday nights. Then the old folk tell stories about long ago, when everything was different and the men went out to fish in rowing boats.

And they make music. Pat Dirane
always has his flute with him, and Moira's
grandfather takes up his fiddle.

And when they play, everyone feels like dancing. Even the cows spin around in circles. The sheep stop bleating, and the donkey kicks up its heels. People always say their music could charm the fish out of the sea, and the mermaids, too. That's how beautiful it is.

The donkey belongs to Moira's father, and its name is Little Brogeen. It helps Moira's father collect peat from the bog.

Once, Moira tried to ride Little
Brogeen. But the donkey wouldn't move
an inch, forwards or backwards. It stood
still and stared straight ahead, pretending
it didn't know what to do.

But the donkey isn't as stupid as it
looks. It knows how to open the gate to
the vegetable garden so it can eat the
lettuce.

Moira has a dog called Abby. Abby is black with white patches, and she's the nicest dog in the world. Abby's job is to watch the goats and make sure they don't run away. She keeps the cats out of the house too. Abby is Moira's best friend.

They often go to the meadow together
and watch the clouds floating past and
the sea gulls wheeling and diving. This
makes Moira and Abby dizzy after a while.
Then they have to look away.

Sometimes they run down to the beach to look for driftwood and unusual shells. Or they walk to the other end of the island. There the cliffs are high and steep, and the waves send up huge fountains of spray as they crash against the rocks. Moira and Abby sit on the highest cliff, and Moira shouts and waves when a fishing boat sails by.

Moira can sit perfectly still, holding out her arms like the branches of a tree. Then little birds come and sit on her hands or on her head. Abby sits beside her, looking perplexed.

Sometimes, when Moira is at school, Abby runs off and stays away all day.

At school Moira often thinks about Abby. She pictures her running with the sheep, barking as loud as she can, and the sheep running down the hill bleating, and Abby scampering after them, enjoying the game.

One day, in the middle of this dream, the teacher said, "Moira, what's seven plus nine minus four?"

Oh dear, thought Moira. Now I'm in trouble!

"Thirteen," muttered Sean.

"Thirteen," said Moira.

"Wrong!" said the teacher. And she made Moira copy out two whole pages of the textbook, for not paying attention.

When Moira came home that day, she saw a note from her mother on the table:

*Gone to Daniel's. Boil some potatoes for yourself, and don't forget to bring the goats into the stable.*

*Love, Mam*

Funny, thought Moira. Why would Mam go to Daniel's?

Daniel lived all alone, right in the middle of the bog, and no one saw much of him. They called him Rusty Daniel in the village, because of his red hair and freckly face.

Moira boiled the potatoes and ate three
helpings, with butter and salt. Then she
went to get the goats. They were all out
on the hillside, eating blackberries. Moira
called and whistled and waved her arms,
but the goats didn't take the slightest
notice. Moira went around to the back of
the house. Oh no! The donkey was in the
vegetable patch. It had opened the gate
again. Everything is going wrong today,
thought Moira. Where on earth is Abby?

Moira got her grandfather's stick from behind the stove and chased Little Brogeen out of the vegetable patch. And she drove the goats down from the hillside. Then she sat on the doorstep and tried to do her homework.

Four goats minus one donkey, plus six cats—that made eleven, didn't it? Oh dear, why did addition and subtraction have to be so difficult? Moira frowned, and chewed the end of her pencil.

Then she saw her mother coming up
the path. She was carrying Moira's little
brother, Brendan. Behind Mam was
someone else . . . Rusty Daniel! And he
was carrying something too.

"It's . . . it's Abby!" Moira gasped.

Moira rushed down the steep path.
"What's wrong?" she said. "What's
happened to Abby?"

Her mother didn't say a word. She just stared out across the meadow. Pat Dirane was herding the sheep. Mam stared at him as if she had never seen anyone herding sheep before.

Abby's whole body was trembling. Her eyes were shut tight. Moira felt Abby's nose. It was hot and dry.

Daniel cleared his throat. "I'm sorry, lass," he said as he trudged past her.

"Tell me what happened!" Moira cried, and her voice was shrill with fear.

"Daniel put out poisoned meat," said
Mam. "Because a fox had been after his
hens. Abby must have eaten some of it."

"Is she going to be all right?" Moira
asked, tugging at her mother's sleeve.

28

Mam shrugged helplessly.

"I'm sorry, lass," Daniel said again. "Really sorry."

They went indoors, and Daniel laid Abby gently on a blanket in front of the stove. Then he stood there, shifting awkwardly from one foot to the other.

Mam dumped Brendan on the chair next to the television, taking no notice of his howls of protest. She hugged Moira and stroked her hair.

"Does this mean she . . . she's going to die?" whispered Moira, looking anxiously at her mother's face.

"I'll buy you a new one, if you like," said Daniel, looking away from Moira as he spoke.

"I don't want a new one!" Moira said. "I want Abby!" And she flung herself at Daniel, punching him and kicking him on the shin.

Daniel turned and went out.

Moira knelt beside Abby, sobbing. She stroked her head and held her tight, pressing her face into Abby's neck. She could hear the dog's heartbeat, pounding then stopping, then pounding again, going much too fast.

Moira's father came in. "I heard what happened," he said, kneeling down next to Abby. He ran his hand gently across Abby's stomach, up and down. He lifted one of her eyelids. And he felt her pulse. Then he stood up and shook his head.

"It looks bad, dearie. Let's just hope she's eaten only a little poison and will pull through. You should keep her legs moving so the poison doesn't stiffen them permanently." Sadly Moira's father shook his head again. When he left, his shoulders were hunched and his head was bowed.

Moira took Abby's head onto her lap. She stroked her very gently, along her back and down her sides, over and over again. And when Abby tried to close her eyes, Moira held them open.

Moira kept talking and talking to Abby. She told her long stories, like the ones the old folk told on Saturday nights. And stories about her own life. And about things she had learned at school, like what makes the tides rise and fall, and how the earth spins as it goes around the sun, and why people on the other side of the world don't hang upside down.

Moira's parents tiptoed out of the
kitchen. Her dad didn't even turn on the
television to watch the weather forecast.
They didn't want any loud noises to startle
Abby. Then Mam accidentally dropped
the soup tureen, and the broken pieces
clattered across the floor. But Abby's ears
didn't even twitch.

Now I know she's dying, thought Moira,
holding her even closer.

Moira buried her face in Abby's coat.
Her mother bent down and kissed her.
"It's late," she said. "We're going to bed
now. I've left you a cup of tea on the
table."

After a while Moira got a bowl of water and a washcloth. She pressed the damp cloth gently against Abby's hot nose, over and over again, until the cloth was nearly dry. Then she wet it again, and pressed it against Abby's nose some more.

The house was getting cold.
Moira opened the door of the stove and
pushed another lump of peat onto the fire.

Moira heard Brendan whimpering in his sleep. And Little Brogeen brayed once. There was no other sound, except for the wind rattling the roof tiles now and then, and the big clock softly ticking away the seconds.

Abby wasn't making a sound either.
She had stopped trembling now and lay
quite still. Her legs were stiff, and Moira
tried to move them gently, as her father
had suggested.

Moira forced Abby to keep her eyes open. She kept whispering stories in her ear, and said, "Don't fall asleep, Abby! Do you hear? Don't fall asleep . . ."

Then Moira herself fell asleep, with her face pressed against Abby's neck and her arm across Abby's back. And she started to dream.

It was a crazy dream, all muddled up. She dreamed she was sailing far out to sea in a fishing boat, to a small island where monks used to live. Then she dreamed she was lying on the warm grass, looking at the sky, and that Abby was there licking her face.

"Stop it," murmured Moira in her sleep.

But Abby wouldn't stop. She kept on licking Moira's face until Moira pushed her away crossly and opened her eyes.

She saw Abby's nose, and Abby's rough tongue coming to lick her again.

"Abby . . ." whispered Moira. "Abby."
Abby tried to stand up, and her brown
eyes looked steadily at Moira.

"Abby," Moira whispered again,
thinking she must still be dreaming.
Outside it was getting light, and the cats
were sitting on the windowsill, looking in.
Abby's water bowl was empty, and Abby
was slowly wagging her tail.

Moira jumped up. "Abby's alive!" she shouted as she ran through the house. "Abby's alive!"

Moira leaped on the sofa, danced on a chair and then on the table. Abby tilted her head to one side and watched in amazement. And then she began to sing, quietly, because she was still so weak, but still loud enough for everyone to hear: "Waaoowaaoo!"

Moira didn't have to go to school that
day. Her father said he would go and see
the teacher later and explain everything.
Moira and her mother took their time
over breakfast. They gave Abby a plate
of Brendan's baby mush and a big bowl
of water.

Later Moira and Abby sat side by side in the meadow and looked up at the sky. They watched the gulls wheeling and diving.

Suddenly Moira stood up. "Can you tell me what seven plus nine minus four makes?" she said, kissing Abby on the nose. "Well, at least we know it's not thirteen," she said with a grin. And Abby pricked up her ears and wagged her tail.

## About the Author

Wolfram Hänel was born in Fulda, Germany. He was going to be a teacher, but instead he began to write plays and stories for children. He lives with his wife and daughter mostly in Hannover, Germany, and sometimes in Kilnarovanagh, a small village in southern Ireland, where this true story actually took place. His other easy-to-read books for North-South include *Lila's Little Dinosaur*, *Mia the Beach Cat*, *The Old Man and the Bear*, and *Jasmine and Rex*.

*About the Illustrator*

Alan Marks was born in London. After training as a graphic designer at the Medway College of Art and Design and the Academy of Art in Bath, he worked for various magazines and newspapers. He lives in Kent, England, with his wife and two daughters. Among the North-South books he has illustrated are two award-winning collections of nursery rhymes, *Over the Hills and Far Away* and *Ring-a-ring O' Roses and a Ding, Dong Bell.*

**Other Easy-to-Read Books
by Wolfram Hänel**

*The Old Man and the Bear*
Illustrated by Jean-Pierre Corderoc'h

*Mia the Beach Cat*
Illustrated by Kirsten Höcker

*The Extraordinary Adventures of an Ordinary Hat*
Illustrated by Christa Unzner-Fischer

*Jasmine and Rex*
Illustrated by Christa Unzner

*Lila's Little Dinosaur*
Illustrated by Alex de Wolf

*The Other Side of the Bridge*
Illustrated by Alex de Wolf